THE BUMBLEBEE AND THE RAM

by

Barry Rudner

Illustrated by Thomas Fahsbender

ISBN 0-925928-03-8

Printed/Published in the U.S.A. by Art-Print &
Publishing Company. Tiny Thought Press is a trademark
and service mark of Art-Print & Publishing Company.
Publisher is located in Louisville, Kentucky 40217
@ 1427 South Jackson St. (502) 637-6870 or
outside Kentucky 1-800-456-3208

Library of Congress Catalog Card Number: 89-81585

To Charlie

11/23-01
TO Kellie
"Bee" yourself
Barry

Once upon a summer morn,
before a bright new day
was born,
Mother Nature played
a trick.
She created for fun --
a flying brick.

She created the bumblebee,
you see.
It was bigger than any bee
should be.

It looked like a flying jelly bean.

It buzzed just like a sewing machine.

She laughed to herself
how funny it was,
as she dressed the bee
in yellow-striped fuzz.

She gave it wings,
wings so small,
it looked like it
couldn't fly at all.

But up from the ground
this bee flew around,
flying from flower
to flower,
humbly tumbling
and bumbling along,
under its very
own power.

The bee waved goodby
as it took to the sky.
It was happy being
a bee.
But all of a sudden
it ran into something
appearing to be
a TV.

5

"OW!" said the bee
as it fell to the ground.
"Who turned off the lights?"

"I did ," the thing grumbled,
"and my name is Ram,
a computer with memory bytes."

"You are not like any goat
I've ever seen. Let's see
if you "BAHH" like
a lamb.
Where are your horns and
hooves," asked the bee,
"if you say that you are
a ram?"

Ram looked at the bee
and laughed aloud
and said, "That is surely
a fact.
But my figures and numbers
tell me that you, should
drop to the ground like
a sack."

"I don't really know
how I fly," said the bee.
"I just flap my wings
like this, you see."

"I don't wish to be
the bringer of doom.
But you should drop
like a lead balloon.
You cannot fly
with your wings
so stubby.
You cannot fly
with your body
so chubby."

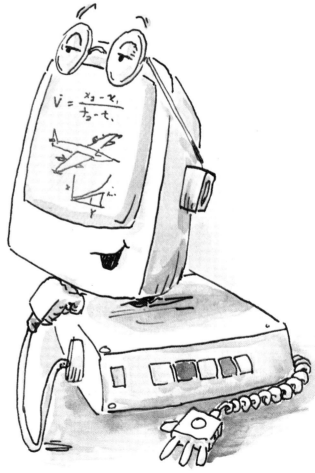

"I'll make you better than ever," said Ram. "You'll truly fly like a bird. All you have to do, bumblebee, is say the magic word."

The bee looked around
for a little assistance.
Mother Nature
looked on from off
in the distance.

She knew to interfere
was something she mustn't,
if the bee wished to be
something it wasn't.

"Okay," said the bee.
"You're welcome to try.
Maybe you're right,
and I really can't fly.
I hope what we're doing
is not a mistake.
And you, my friend,
are not a big fake."

"Great!" Ram exclaimed.
"We have no time to waste.
There's a lot to repair.
So let us make haste."

"The program to follow
has already been keyed.
Just do what I say, and
that's all you'll need."

"First we'll start off
by doing some trimming.
You'll take to the air like
a fish takes to swimming."

"Your wings, we'll build them
straight and long.
We'll give you two more
to make them strong."

"For sound we'll hang speakers
between each wing.
Instead of buzzing, your wings
will sing."

"We'll give you twin jets
to give you more power.
Now you will rocket
from flower to flower."

"For speed on each leg
we'll give you a wheel.
When you take-off
your wheels will squeal."

"Your stinger, your stinger
is the place my feller,
for us to attach a shiny
propeller."

The bumblebee looked
in Ram's green screen
and said aloud, "I see
what you mean.
I'm faster,
stronger,
more powerful
and lean.
I'm a flying
machine.
I'm a supersonic
bean."

Ram, too, was pleased
with what it saw
and boasted aloud,"You
have no more flaws.
Fix your helmet and goggles
and wrap your scarf tight.
For now you'll give
new meaning to flight."

"CONTACT!" was yelled.
The propeller was wound.
The jets were fired
with a deafening sound.

The brakes were turned off,
the bee hit the throttle
and shot down the runway
like fizz from a bottle.

All of a sudden,
with a sputter of smoke,
the propeller quit spinning,
the jet engines broke.

Instead of flying
and rocketing around,
the bumblebee nosedived
into the ground.

After the bumblebee
came to a halt,
Ram shrugged and said,
"It's not my fault.
I don't understand
why you did not fly.
Try again! Try again!
Again, you should try!"

"No!" buzzed the bee
in disgust to Ram.
"I am much better off
just being who I am."

With that, the bee started
to rip off its gear,
and then out of nowhere
Mother Nature appeared.
"I hope you have learned
a valuable lesson."

"I have. I have," was the bee's
confession.
"It was never impossible
for me to fly, only for Ram
to tell me why."

25

Mother Nature then patted
the bee on the head.
She turned her attention
to Ram instead.
"Is there something else
you would like to improve,
before I make the very
last move?"

"Well," said Ram,
"if you don't mind.
There's a fault or two
in you I find."

"Oh, really?" she asked.
"Maybe that's true.
There's just one thing
that I wish to do."

With a flick of her wrist
and a very slight tug,
she pulled from the wall
the electrical plug.

About the Author . . .
Barry Rudner, a Pisces-born twin, was born thirty five
years ago in Detroit where he can still be found to be
growing up.

About the Illustrator . . . . .
Thomas Fahsbender is a sculptor from
New Preston, Connecticut who has never found
a comfortable pair of dress shoes.

About the Publisher . . . . .
Art-Print & Publishing Company (Tiny Thought
Press) would like to hear from
you. Please call us at 1-800-456-3208
and tell us what you think about
"The Bumblebee and The Ram." We are committed
to the enjoyment of children, parents
and grandparents alike.

Other Tiny Thoughts . . . . .

The Littlest Tall Fellow (@ Local Stores)

The Wind and The Skyscraper

The Statue and The Gift

The Nightmare

The Sound of One Hand Clapping

The Ring

The Handstand

Nonsense

Plus others . . . . .